ED YOUNG

Seven Blind Mice

PUFFIN BOOKS

One day seven blind mice were surprised
to find a strange Something by their pond.
"What is it?" they cried, and they all ran home.

On Monday, Red Mouse went first to find out.

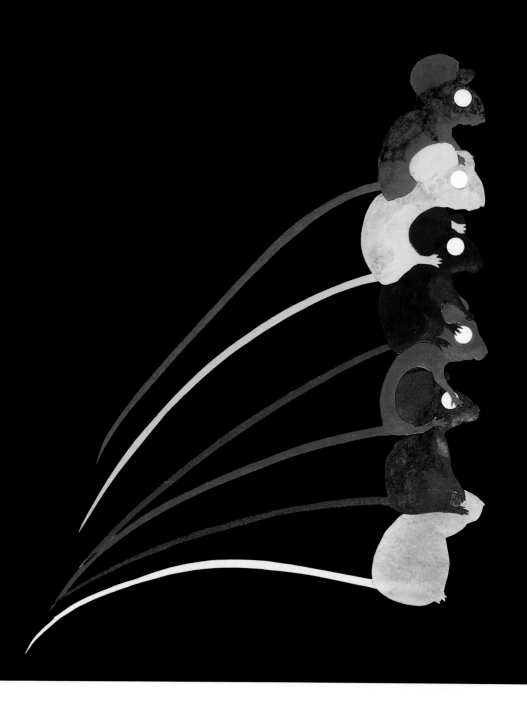

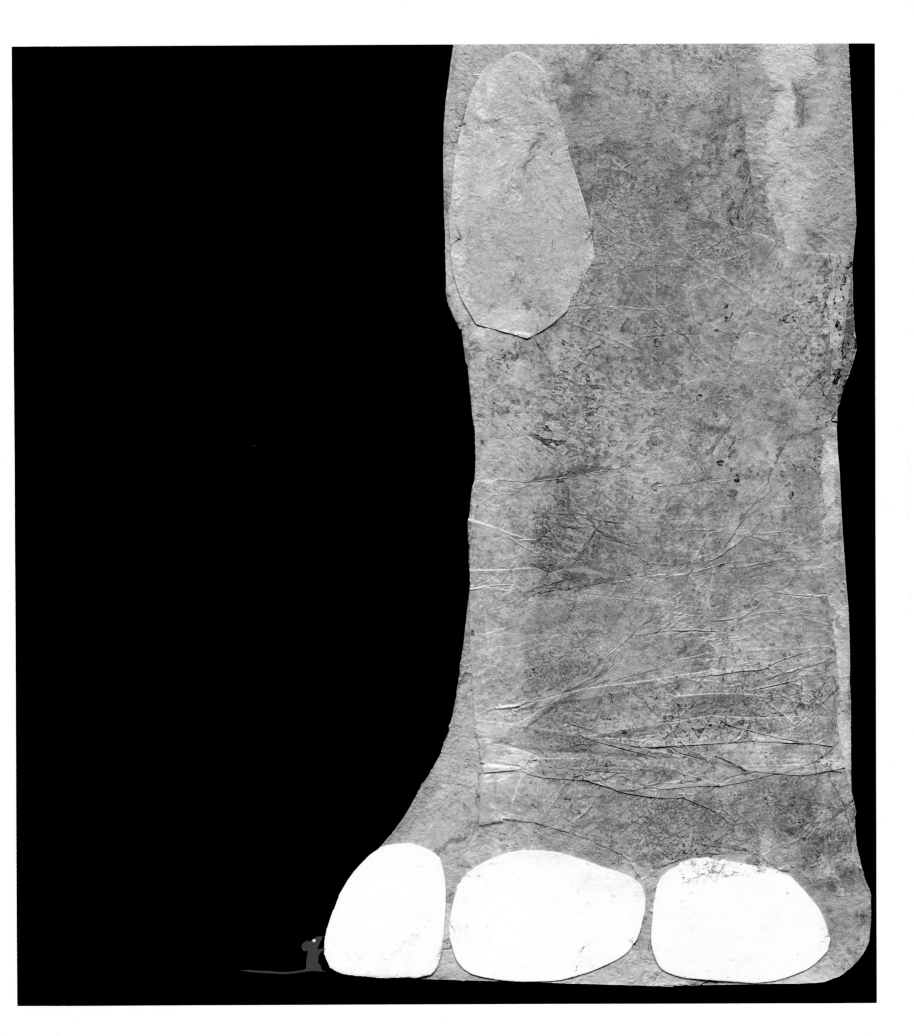

"It's a pillar," he said.
  No one believed him.

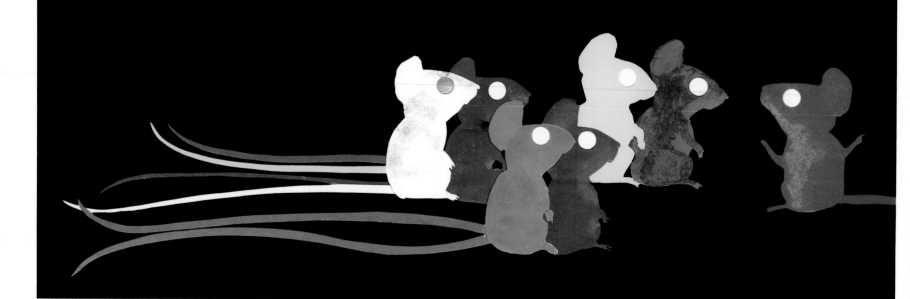

On Tuesday, Green Mouse set out.
He was the second to go.

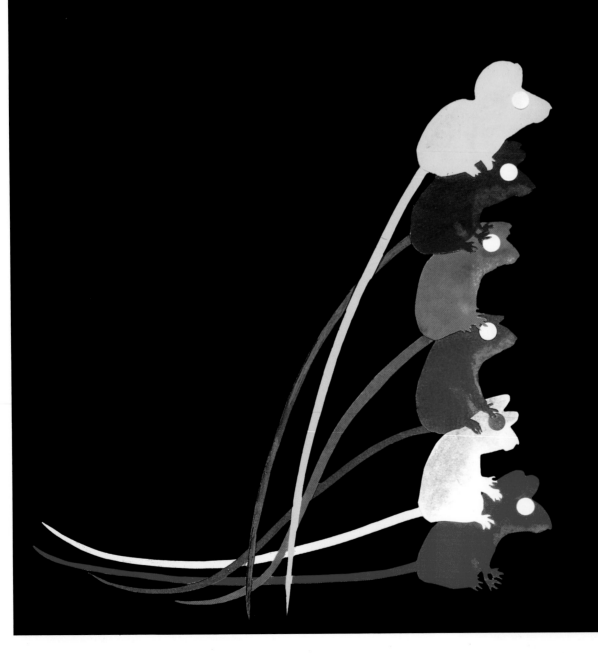

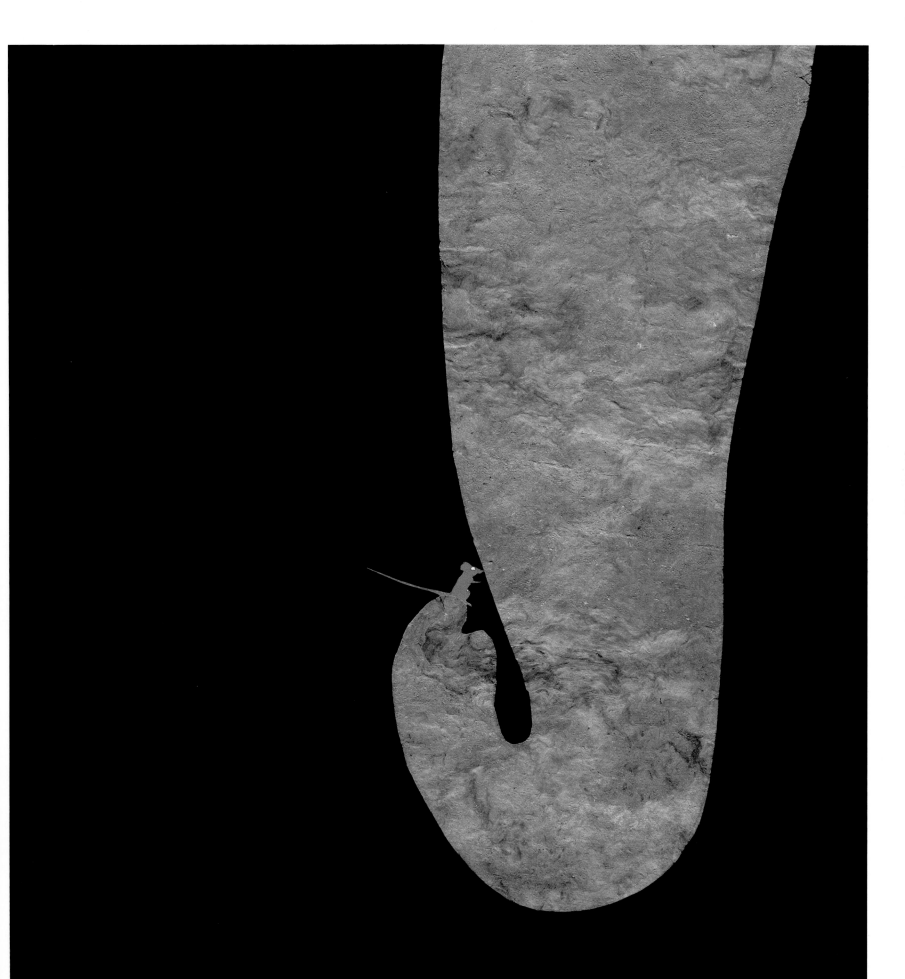

"It's a snake," he said.

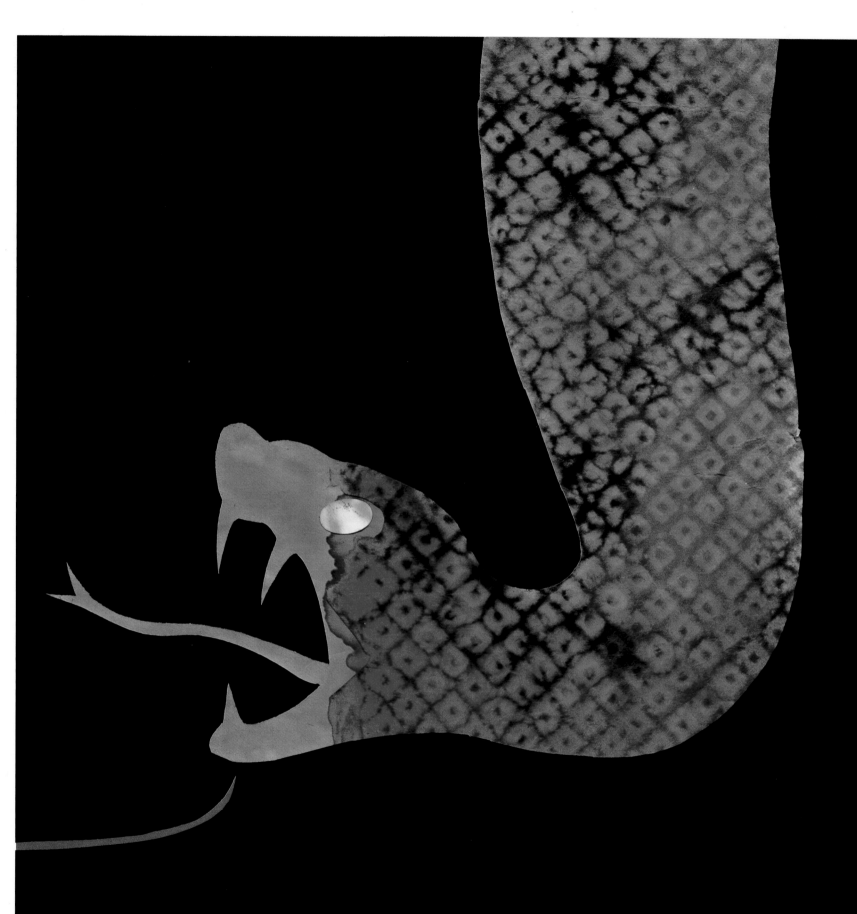

"No," said Yellow Mouse on Wednesday.

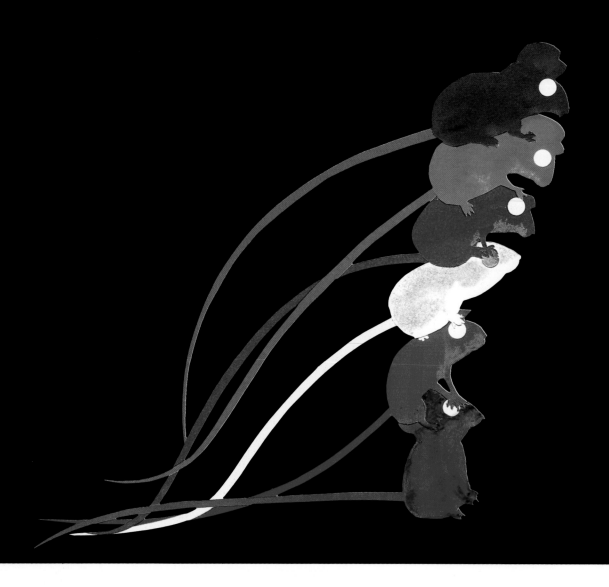

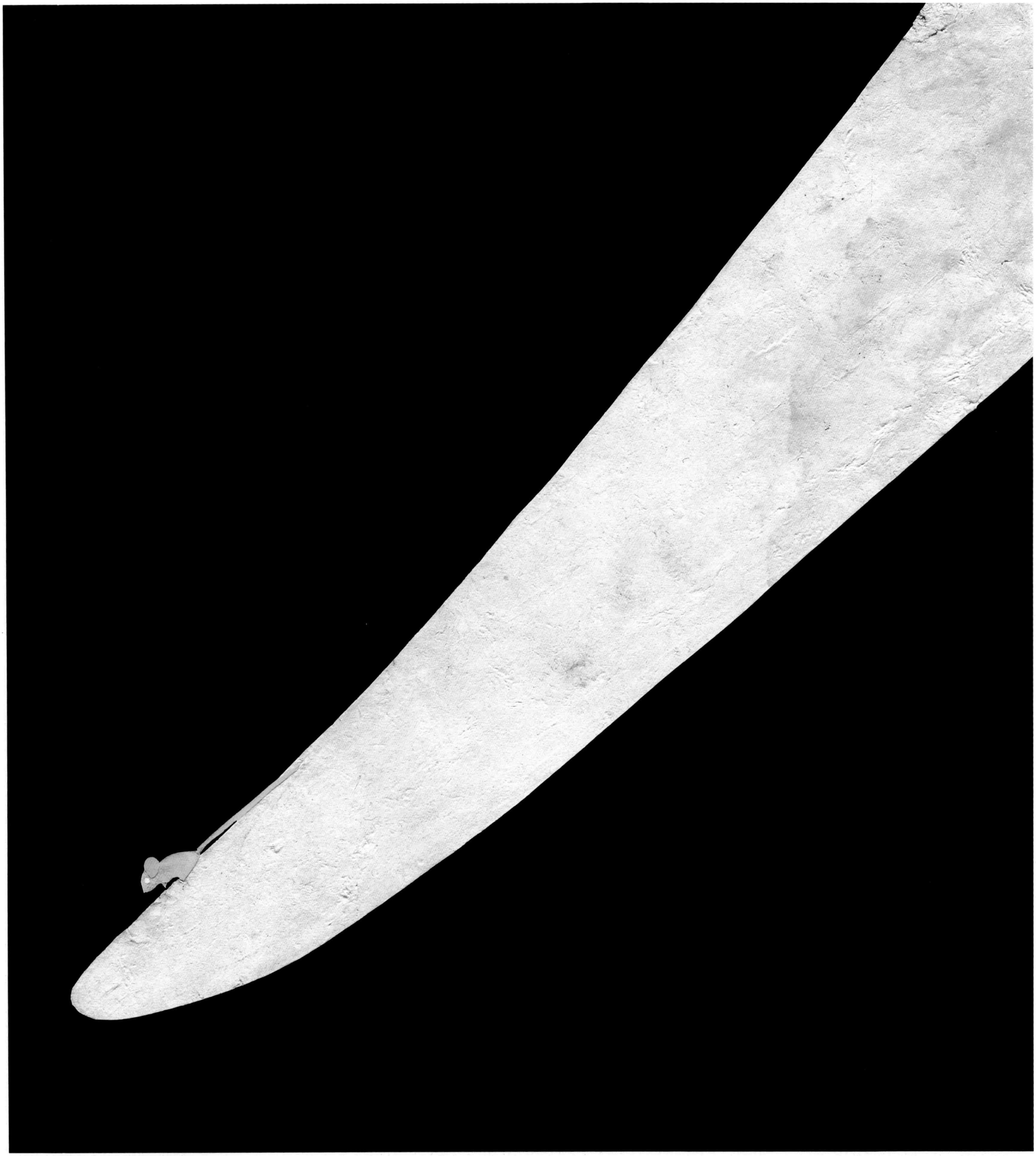

"It's a spear."
He was the third in turn.

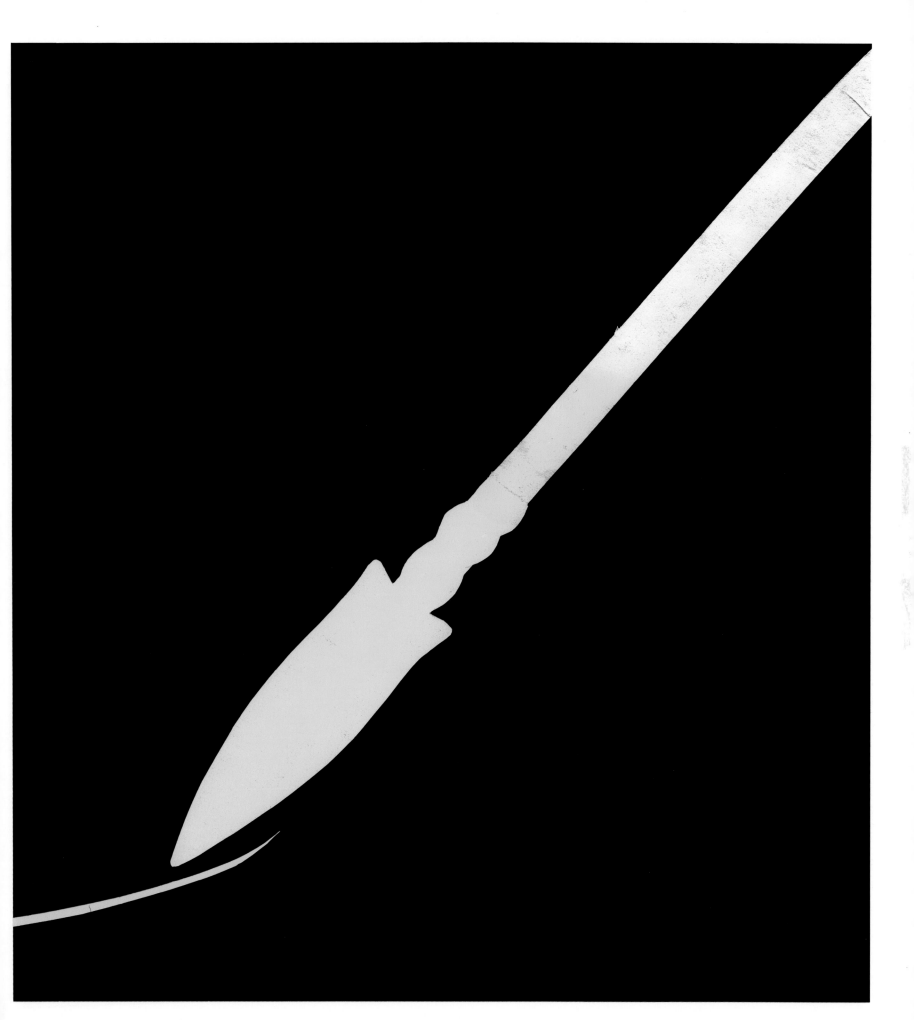

The fourth was Purple Mouse.
He went on Thursday.

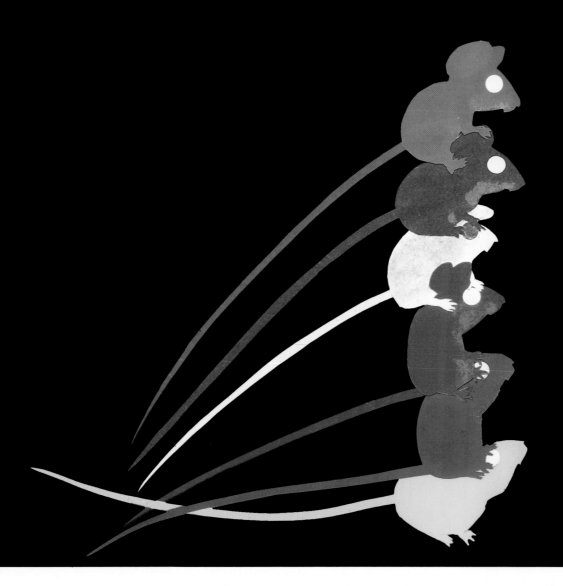

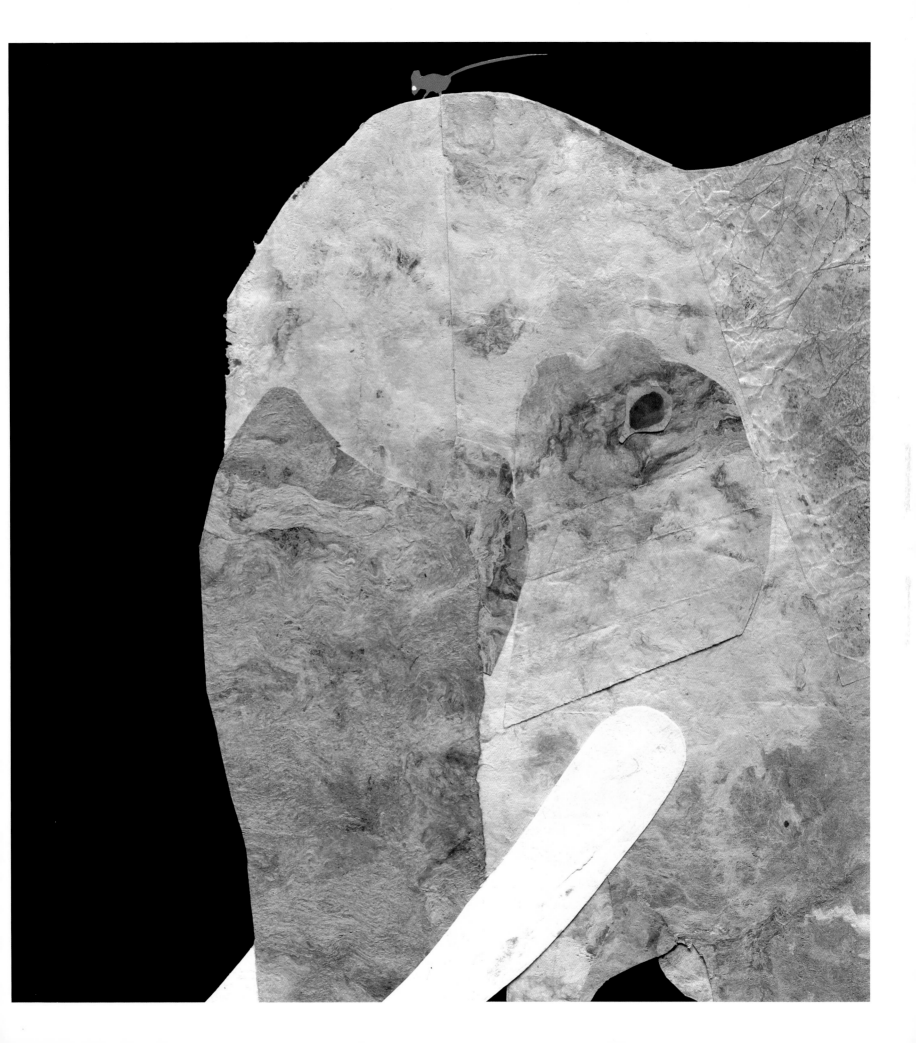

"It's a great cliff," he said.

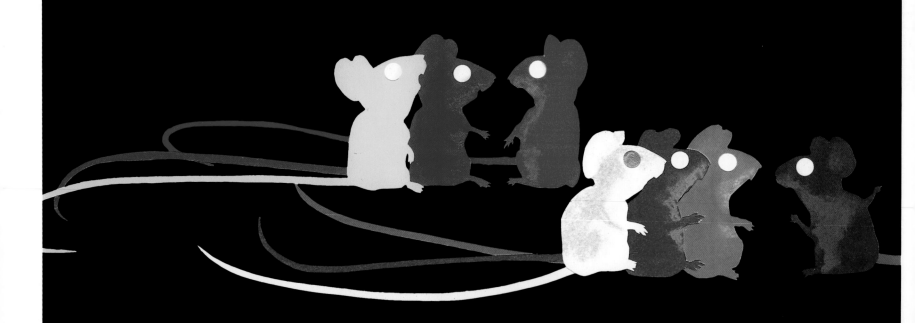

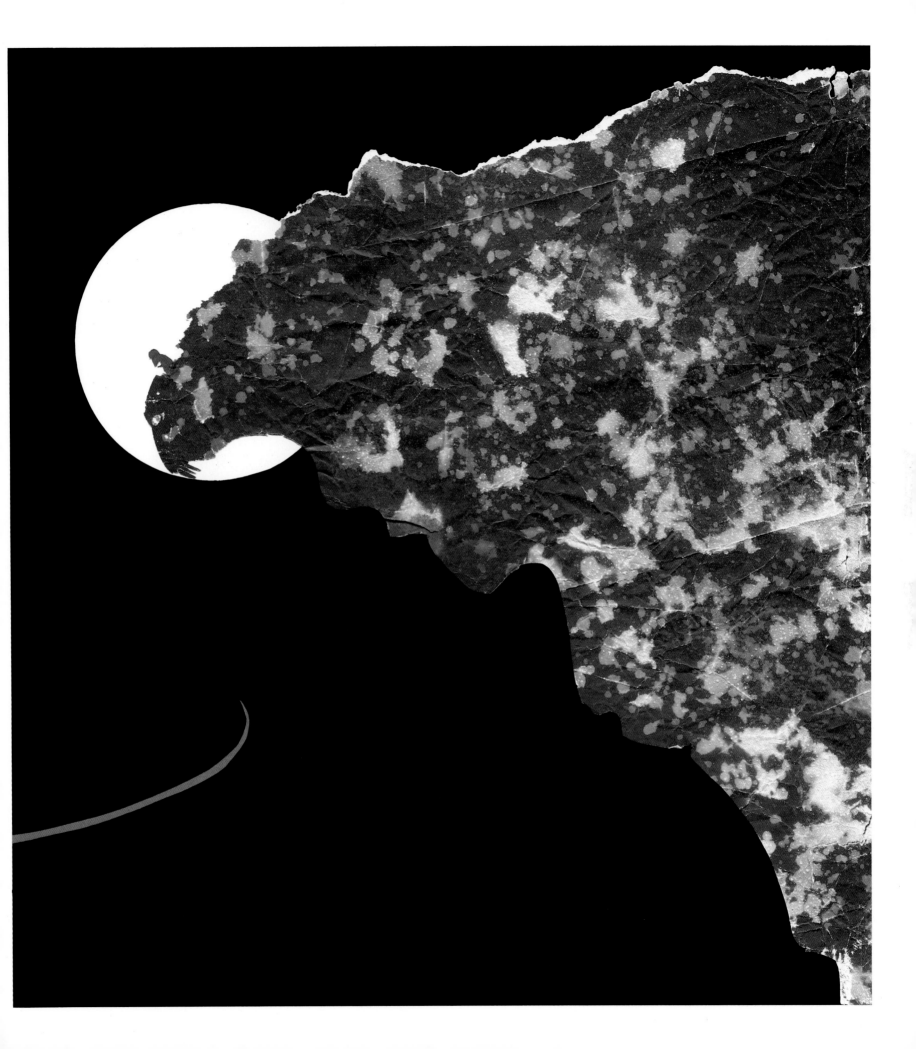

Orange Mouse went on Friday, the fifth to go.

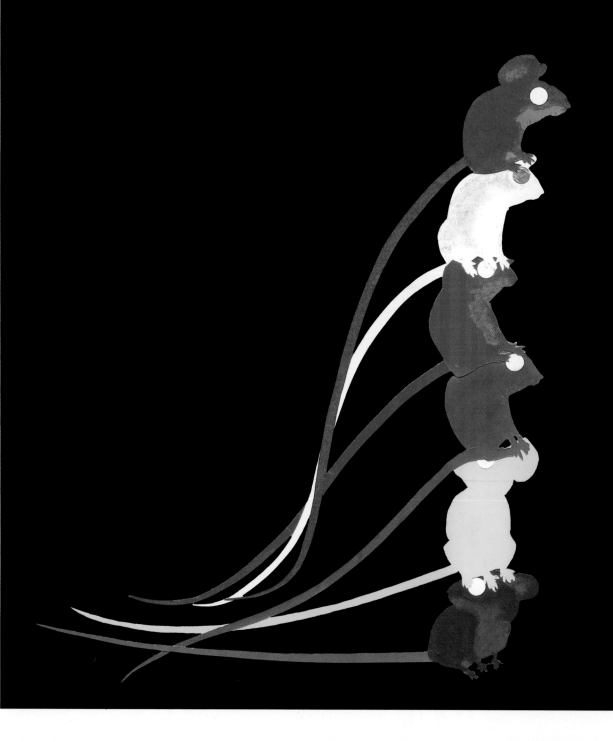

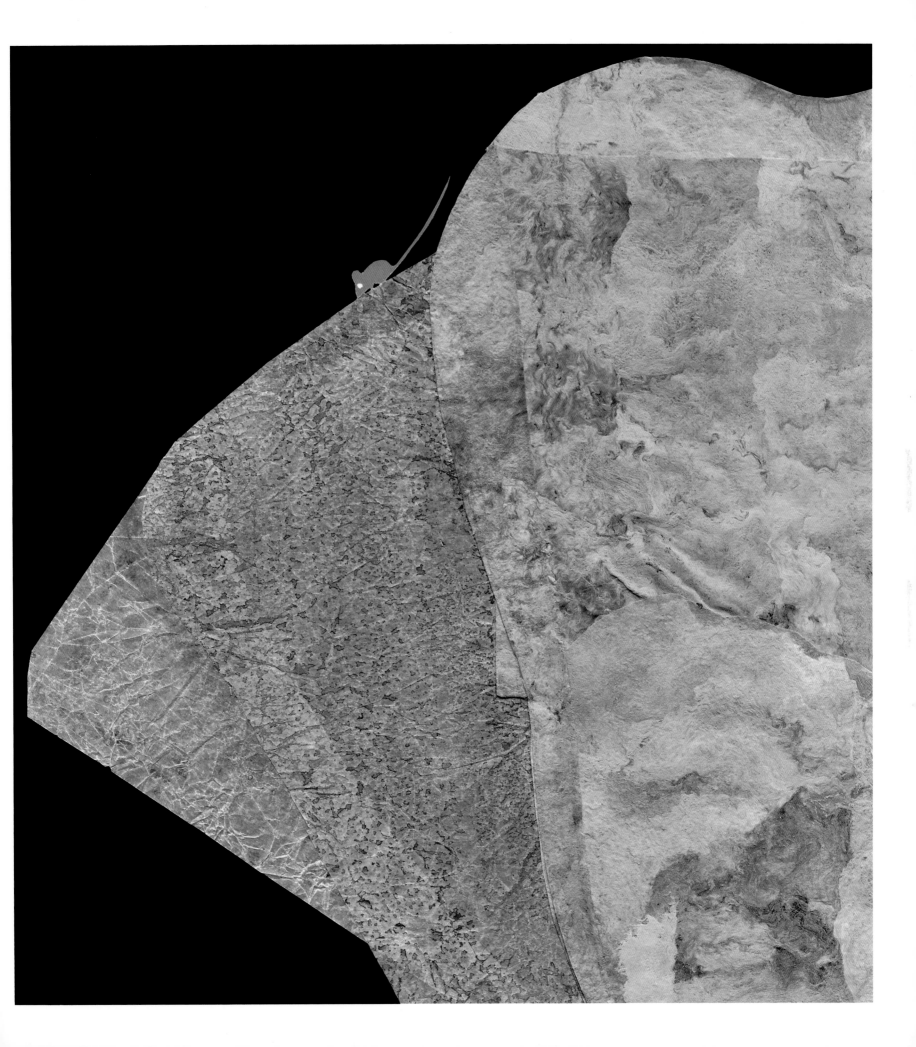

"It's a fan!" he cried. "I felt it move."

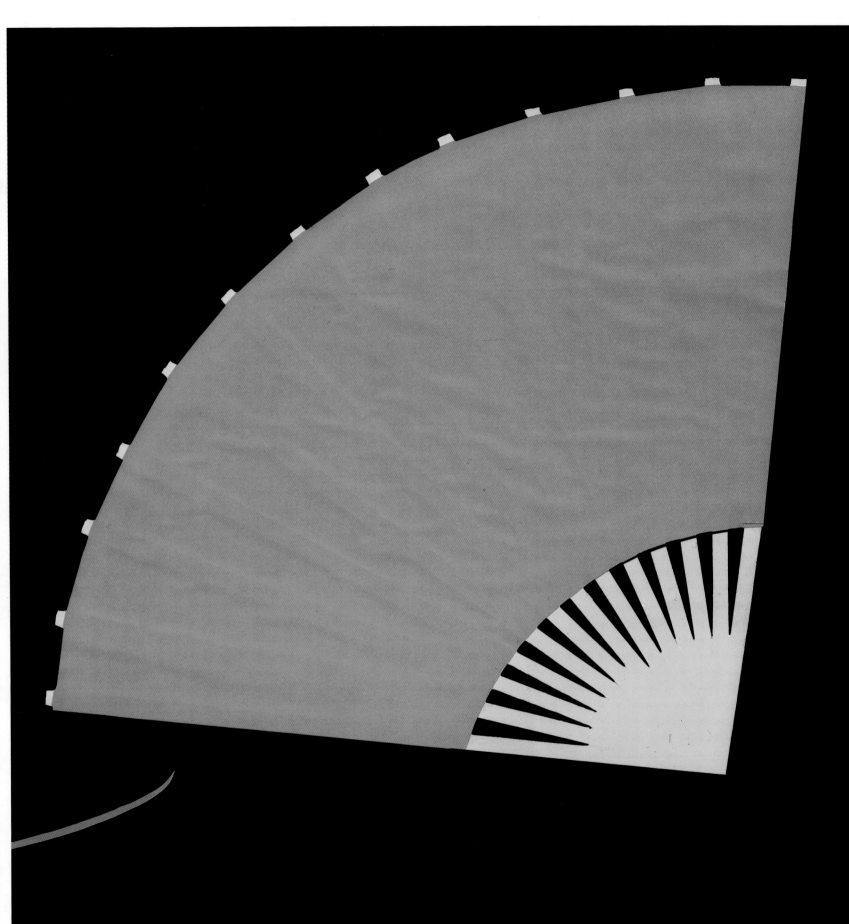

The sixth to go was Blue Mouse.

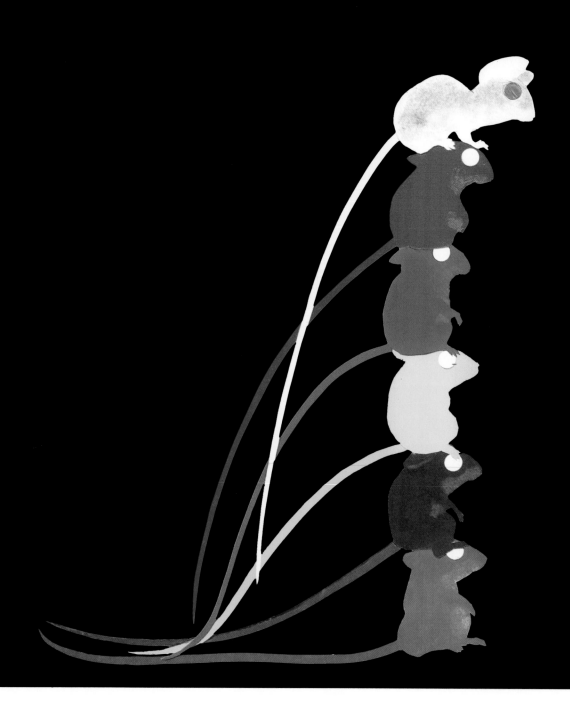

He went on Saturday and said,
"It's nothing but a rope."

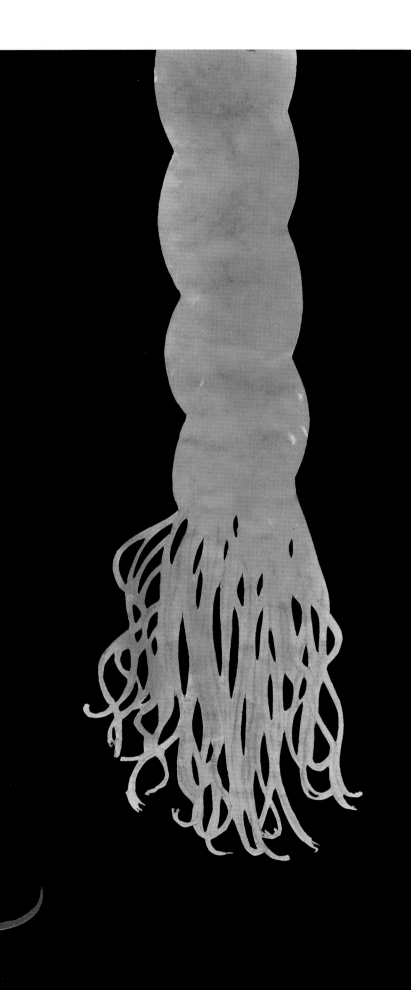

But the others didn't agree.
They began to argue.
"A snake!" "A rope!" "A fan!" "A cliff!"

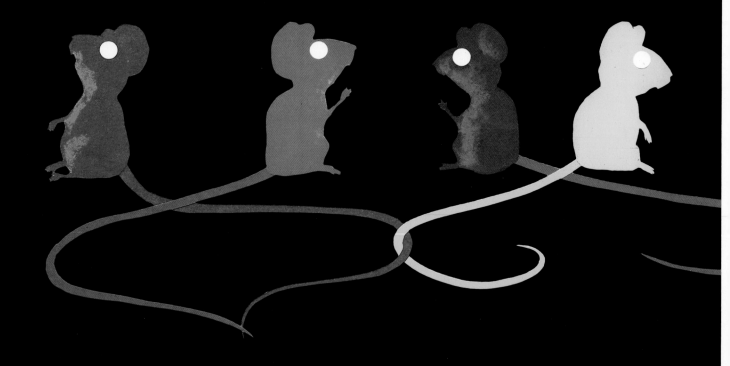

Until on Sunday, White Mouse,
the seventh mouse,
went to the pond.

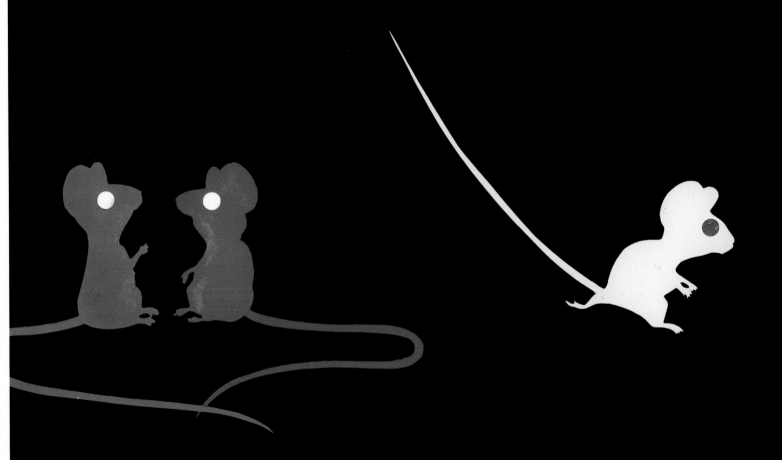

When she came upon the Something, she ran up one side, and she ran down the other. She ran across the top and from end to end.

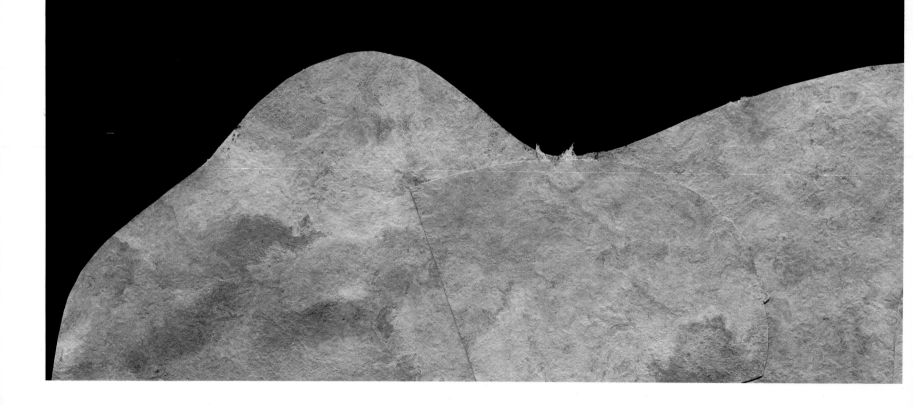

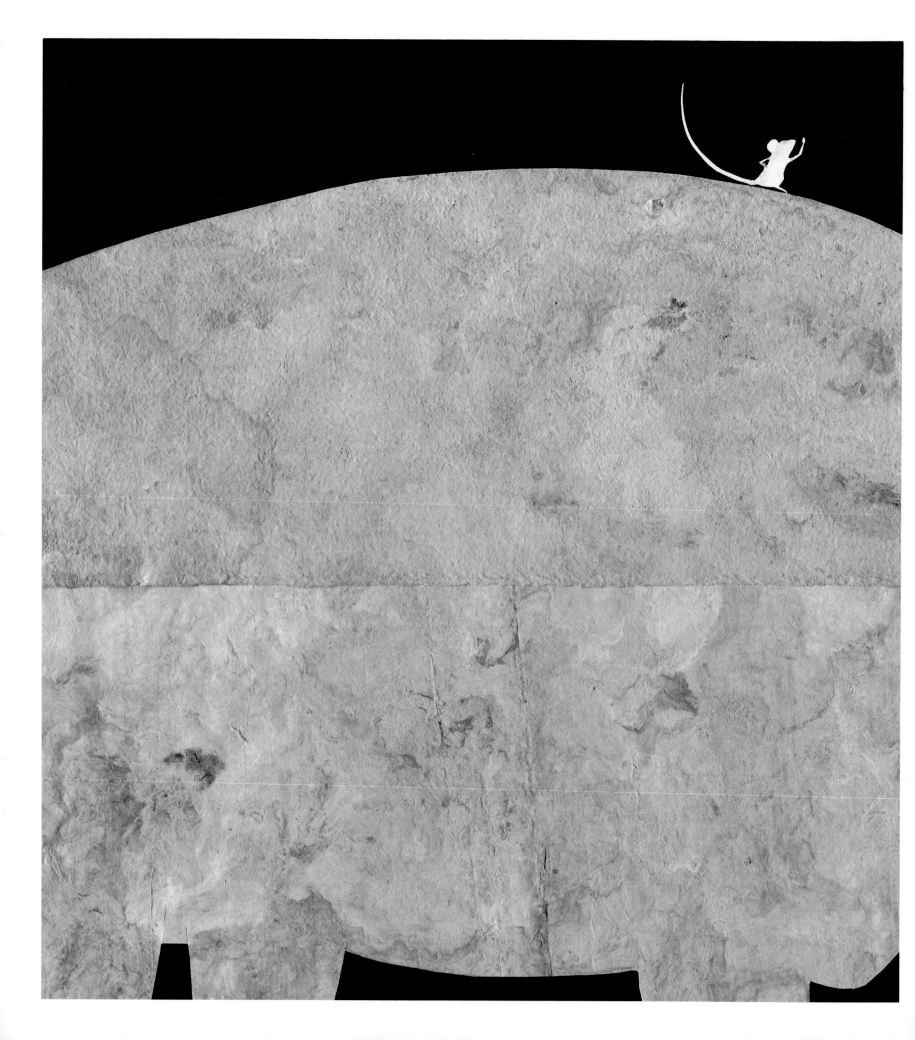

"Ah," said White Mouse. "Now, I see. The Something is

as sturdy as a pillar,
supple as a snake,
wide as a cliff,
sharp as a spear,
breezy as a fan,
stringy as a rope,
but altogether the Something is...

an elephant!"

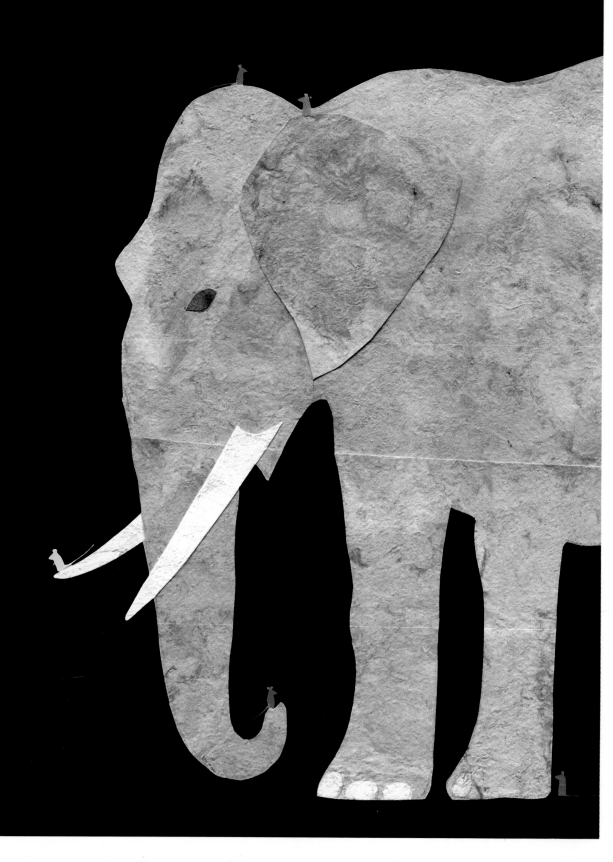

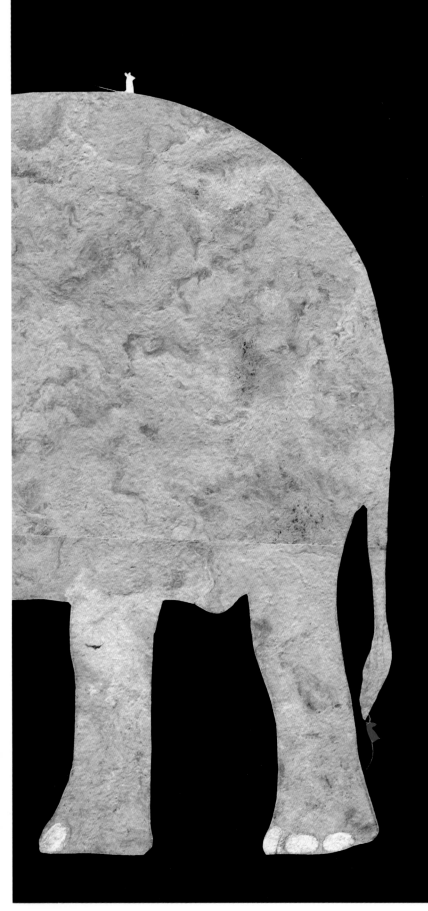

And when the other
mice ran up one side
and down the other,
across the Something
from end to end,
they agreed.
Now they saw, too.

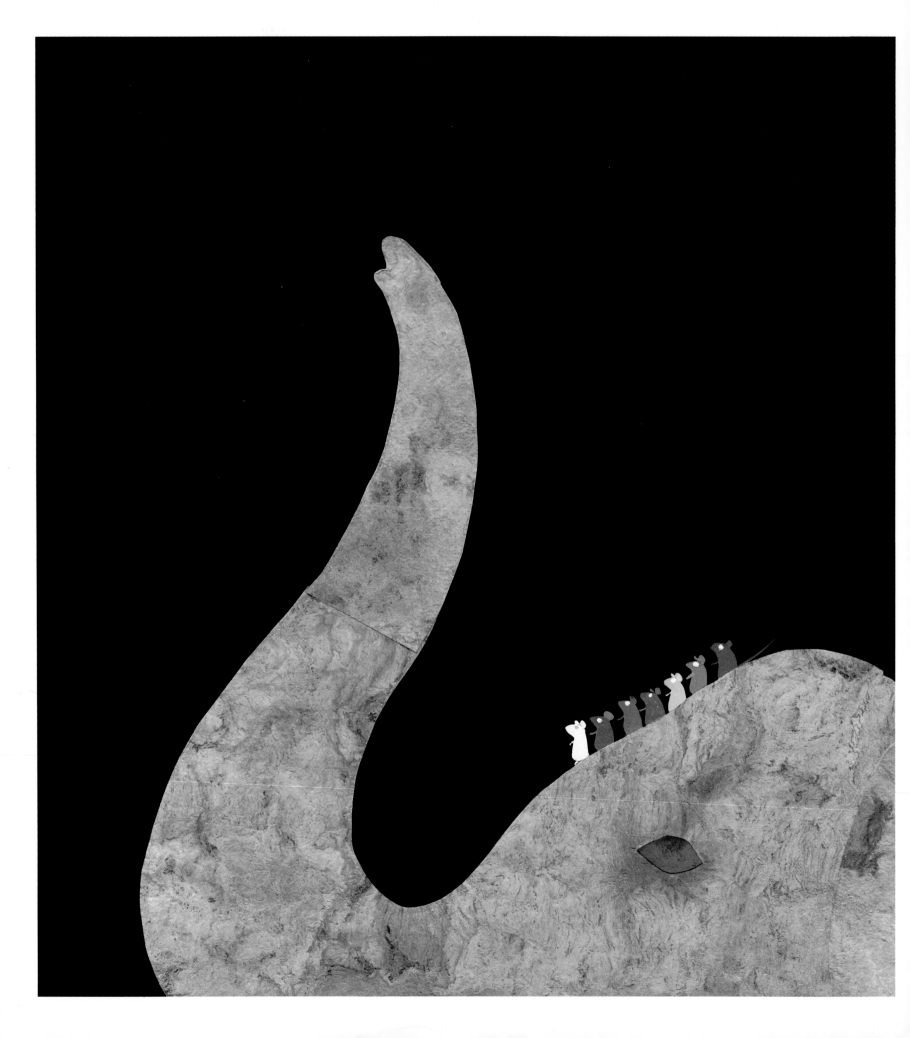

The Mouse Moral:
Knowing in part may make a fine tale,
but wisdom comes from seeing the whole.

To Wang Kwong-Mei, 艾耐哥哥
who opened my eyes to the joy
of knowledge and wisdom
in those trying years.

PUFFIN BOOKS
Published by the Penguin Group
Penguin Putnam Books for Young Readers,
345 Hudson Street, New York, New York 10014, U.S.A.
Penguin Books Ltd, 80 Strand, London WC2R ORL, England
Penguin Books Australia Ltd, Ringwood, Victoria, Australia
Penguin Books Canada Ltd, 10 Alcorn Avenue, Toronto, Ontario, Canada M4V 3B2
Penguin Books (N.Z.) Ltd, 182-190 Wairau Road, Auckland 10, New Zealand
Penguin Books Ltd, Registered Offices: Harmondsworth, Middlesex, England

First published in the United States of America by Philomel Books,
a division of The Putnam & Grosset Group, 1992
Published by Puffin Books, a division of Penguin Putnam Books for Young Readers, 2002

10

THE LIBRARY OF CONGRESS HAS CATALOGED THE PHILOMEL EDITION AS FOLLOWS:
Young, Ed.   Seven Blind Mice/Ed Young.   p.   cm.
Adaptation of: The Blind men and the elephant.
Summary: Retells in verse the Indian fable of the blind men discovering different parts of an
elephant and arguing about its appearance. The illustrations depict the blind arguers as mice.
ISBN 0-399-22261-8
[1. Fables. 2. Elephants—Folklore. 3. Folklore—India. 4. Stories in rhyme.] I. Blind men and
the elephant. II. Title. PZ8.3.Y786SE 1991 398.24'5961'0954—dc20 [E] 90-35396 CIP AC

Puffin Books ISBN 0-698-11895-2   Manufactured in China